The Adventure of Moet The Blind Cat

By Dr. Emily Shotter

Chapter 1

Moet lifted her head sleepily from the hard floor. She had been dreaming of a forever home again. They must be so wonderful, with food, soft beds and toys, cuddles and strokes and endless chin rubs. She put her head down again, her eyes glanced around the empty cage.

She had arrived here with four litter-mates , all pretty fluffy Persian kittens, with big wide hopeful eyes and boundless energy. Moet was the only cream coloured kitten, the rest being tabby or smoky grey. She had long cotton-wool type fur, big blue eyes and little pink nose on her slightly flattened face. She was a pretty girl, full of life and happiness and bounced happily around with her litter mates in those early days. They had played and had so much fun, but as the others were adopted, one by one, Moet had become more withdrawn and spent more and more of her time sleeping, just waiting for the next human hands to reach in and take her away to a better life. She had been on her own for a whole month now.

The worst thing was, though, that Moet didn't feel well. She had been sneezing for some weeks now and her nose was often congested, and her eyesight had become a little fuzzy. The humans didn't seem to care, however, and went about their daily business, usually talking and drinking coffee. Every now and then, they did the rounds to shove the sparse food and water rations into every cage before resuming their idle chatter.

Beyond her wire prison were other animals in similar cages, different sizes, stacked on top of one another. Two with cats, another with kittens, two with puppies, and one with hamsters, another with rabbits and a few with birds. The area next to Moet's cage was stacked with tanks of brightly coloured fish of different sizes and shapes, swimming back and forth endlessly. Moet loved to peek out of her cage and watch the fish for hours. Their colours and swooshing motion providing much of the day's entertainment. Most of the huge interior of the dark, dingy shop was filled with supplies. Food, toys for all sorts of pets, beds, cages, carriers, scratching posts, fancy collars, name tags for engraving and much more. The shop smelled musty and unkempt. Disinfectant mixed with faeces was the stench for the morning before the shop opened, but by the afternoon the musty smell had returned from overflowing litter trays, uncleaned dog poo, stale sawdust and old food. Despite all the animals, there wasn't much noise. Every time a new batch of puppies came in, the barking and yapping dominated the shop, but as they became weaker and more subdued by the lack of care and food, the barks died down and, just like the kittens, they spent most of their time sleeping or staring blankly out of their own enclosures.

Moet had been there for almost three months and the time passed slowly with nothing to play with and not enough food to eat. Her own wire cage was small and perched just a foot or so off the ground on a wooden ledge. She had been in one of the prized window cages when she had first arrived with her littermates, where people passing by could see them and be lured in to buy, or in most cases, just a cursory look or stroke. But since the others had been adopted, she had become sick, Moet had been moved to the shop interior. Even in her window cage, the floor had been hard, the water bowl empty, the food tasteless and dry and no toys or beds had been provided. All that was in the cats' and kittens' cages in the shop, were litter boxes, since the owners became tired of spilled water and dirty bedding. They decided that the most convenient approach – for them – was to provide nothing.

In her new cage, the conditions were worse. Instead of a hard floor, this one was a wire mesh, which was painful on her delicate pink pads. The food and water bowls were usually empty and her litter box was overflowing, something that the owners seemed reluctant to deal with.

It was mealtime and Moet heard the cage doors around the pet shop being opened one by one and bowls were deposited. She was always the last to be fed because as the mean humans kept saying "she's sick anyway, so she won't be around for much longer and nobody's gonna want her." Still, Moet held her head high and kept her happy disposition. The cage door opened, and a hand thrust down a tiny bowl of food. Moet ate the dry, unappetising food hungrily, finishing it far too quickly and her tummy wasn't nearly full. The water dish had the remains of a tiny pool of stale, almost flaky water. Moet tried to drink it, turning her head away in disappointment.

She tried to play with a piece of plastic from the dish that had come loose, but that didn't offer much entertainment. After a while, she went to lie next to the litter box, the sides of which she pressed herself again, feeling secure.

Months passed. As Moet opened her eyes each morning to watch the fish and wait for her food, the bright colours and objects in the pet shop became fuzzier and fuzzier. One day, a few months later, she could see only shadows and light. She blinked her eyes, which had become cloudy-looking and blank, but the colours didn't return and even the fuzzy shapes seemed to have merged into one large blob of shadow. She walked over to the food bowl for some comfort. It was empty.

More weeks passed, and Moet became sicker and more withdrawn. Then one day, she woke up and the blobs of shadow were gone and in their place was darkness. By this time her happy disposition was waning. She lay down weakly.

But Moet's time wasn't over.

Chapter 2

Everything happened so suddenly. There was a lot of shouting and rushing around and Moet could hear the panic in the humans' voices. She heard the word 'fire' and the sound of cage doors opening and animals being put into carriers and boxes. Her cage door was the last to be opened and Moet waited to be grabbed, crouching at the back of her cage. A rough hand reached in for her and she cowered away. The hand disappeared for a few seconds and Moet took her chance, she jumped out of the cage and landed on the floor. "Leave her," a voice said, "she's gonna die anyway, so who cares?"

Moet froze. Despite having spent her early life observing the pet shop in great detail, she had been blind for a long time and being at ground level and out of the cage was unfamiliar. It was a big new world and she could see nothing. She took a few tentative steps, using her whiskers and hearing to guide her. The smell of smoke lingered in the air nearby so she walked away from it as quickly as she could, stumbling here and there until the smell of fresh air filled her nostrils. Ahhh, the sweet smell of the great outdoors. She inched her way towards it, hugging the walls to help her find her way.

Once outside she was overwhelmed. She stopped, tilting her head this way and that trying to fix her location. There were so many sounds and smells coming from all directions. She could hear voices, unsure if they were the people from the shop. Would they bother to look for her? Or wouldn't they care knowing how sick she was and at least, they didn't have to concern themselves about her wellbeing any more. She walked a little further. Sounds of cars rushing by, making scary noises propelled her to walk as close to shop walls as she could. Birds chirping in the trees, the feel of the wind rippling through her fur, and the warmth of the sun on her back. Despite not knowing what lay ahead, Moet was free.

Moet wandered carefully and slowly away from the voices and cars that seemed to speed by and disappear off into the distance. She set off, trying to navigate a path for herself that would lead to safety and salvation. As she walked, the world became quieter and the smells changed. She could hear birds in trees, the sounds of laughter muffled and far away, occasional footsteps passing by and even a dog barking. She stopped regularly to take stock, to try and gauge her location. But it was not good, she didn't know where she was going and how to find food, water and shelter. What's more, walking wasn't easy as her paws were sore from being in the wire cage for so long. Occasionally, she bumped into things, banged her nose on something she hadn't sensed, or tripped up. She tried to be careful to check where she was putting each paw as she travelled slowly onwards, but it was tiring, and Moet already felt like she'd been walking for hours. She paused to rest and felt the pangs of hunger in her belly that made it hard to keep going.

After a while, she stopped and sniffed the air. She had been stumbling along for some time and her paws were tender and her fur had gathered dirt and dust. She had been walking towards a residential area and tripped up and down pavements as she moved onwards, passing fences, walls, gates and doorways, but nothing had grabbed her attention, until now. She could smell the unmistakable aroma of food.

Moet was starving and her mouth dry. Her eyes, which had begun to decay several days ago and had started to become painful. She had stopped every now and then to try and sniff out a puddle to

take a drink from, but there had been nothing and the sun was scorching. She tentatively walked up to the doorway where the delicious smell was coming from. She let out a small meow and waited. Nothing. She meowed again, as loudly as her little lungs would allow. Then she scratched on the door. It opened and a loud voice shouted at her. "Get out of here!". Moet meowed pitifully again. The voice shouted at her, and she heard movement of feet coming towards her. She didn't waste another second, stumbling, bumping her head and scratching her ear on something sharp, she ran off, only stopping when she had run out of energy.

Moet found another doorway that was quiet and had some soft grass inside and a bush to shelter underneath. She crawled in, exhausted, and defeated after a long and eventful day and curled up for a nap.

She slept fitfully and for only a short time. The hunger pangs waking her and the feeling of thirst overwhelming. She left her hiding place and sniffed again. This place had grass and plants; it was damper than the other doorways she had passed. She searched around a little finding a plant pot in a saucer, which was filled with water! The drink never tasted so sweet. Although tinged with bits of soil and far from pure, she drank greedily. She lapped it up until it was all gone, then returned to her napping spot, too tired to search for food.

Moet slept again but her will was draining away. The air cooled a little, signalling to her that it was night-time. She crept deeper into the bush for protection – she had no strength for conflict or even to defend herself against whatever might be out there. She curled up into a tight ball for shelter and comfort, to protect herself from the unseen harm she might come to out there in a huge dark world. She was lost in a place filled with mean people and, worst of all, no food. Her stomach had been empty for so long, it had stopped reminding her to eat. She finally managed to fall asleep. Although hungry, she no longer cared whether she might wake up.

Chapter 3

A noise startled her and she cowered in her hiding spot. Footsteps came out of the door; daintier than the feet that had tried to kick her yesterday. They clip-clopped past her and out of the outer gateway and off into the distance. She moved slowly and heavily and tried to stand. She wobbled over to the saucer. It was dry. She went around the rest of the area slowly and found another saucer to drink from. When the earthy water was all gone, she nibbled at some of the grass next to her. It wasn't nourishing or tasty, but it was something to fill her stomach. And she needed to go on and find food desperately as she didn't have much time left. Perhaps it would have been better to have stayed with the mean pet shop people. At least there was food some of the time. But her fate would not have been a good one if she had. Those that got sick were often left to die or thrown into the garbage. Not knowing if she would make it another day, she was at least free, and this would be a comfortable and peaceful resting place.

After a small meal of grass, Moet left the nice garden area and wandered on down past the row of doorways . She trembled each time she came to a new entrance, the memory of her previous experience fresh in her mind, but hunger drove her to try. The next doorway didn't seem promising, it smelled dusty and neglected, so she moved on. At each entrance, she stepped up to the door and meowed as loudly as she could, scratched at the doors and waited patiently. After several unsuccessful doorways, there were no more to explore. Now what? She stepped toward the edge of the pavement and put a paw down onto the road.

A car came rumbling down the road and she pulled her paw back fast. She had heard cars after she had left the pet shop but had no

idea what they were. They would approach, angrily, fly by at speed and then go off into the distance. They sounded mean and scary, so best not to try and interrupt their hurried journeys.

She turned her head in both directions a few times. There were no noises, so she stepped out and walked until she came to the pavement on the opposite side. Once up on this side she found there were lots more doorways to explore. She started at one end, and trundled on heavily with her sore paws and rumbling tummy. She tentatively inched into each entryway and dragged herself towards the doors to meow. By now her walk was laboured. She lay down every now and then to rest, she stumbled on from door to door, and gathered all of her energy to meow as her belly tied itself in painful knots and the harsh sun beat down on her grimy fur, sapping more and more energy. She had not had the strength to wash her long fur since the morning before she had left the pet shop. As it got dirtier and more matted, the task of grooming would have required several dishes of food and water and perhaps a helping human hand; a luxury she didn't have. Eventually she no longer had the strength to scratch at the doors and even when an angry voice answered and shooed her away, she could not run. She simply turned, with great effort, and dragged herself to the next door, in the hope that somebody would give her just a little food.

When she had reached the other end of the street, and with nothing to show for her efforts, she hung her head and lay down again. But there was at least the prospect of the lovely cool bush in the garden, with the grass and the human with the clip-clop footsteps. This was where she wanted to finally rest.

She put a paw down to cross, but she was slow and when a car came speeding towards her, she froze. She tried with all of her might to move faster, but her legs just wouldn't respond. Moet dragged her body and heard a horrible screeching sound. She stopped moving, closed her sightless eyes and held her stance. The car stopped inches from her face. She roused herself from her freeze and crawled on, the effort showing in her laboured gait, until she reached the other side. The car moved off slowly with a voice coming from it "stupid cat!". As it went off into the distance, she dragged herself closer to the doorways, fur standing on end. She would not cross that road again.

Moet was a long way from her haven and resting place. That doorway was at the end of this long stretch and it was going to take a huge effort to make it. Her experience with the car had drained her remaining energy. She lay down; the favoured bush was just too far.

The nap was short, and a loud yowl made her jerk her head up.
The sounds were only too familiar and Moet's fur pricked up and
her body tensed. A large ginger tom was crouched opposite
her, eyes wide and fierce, fluff puffed out and claws at the
ready. Though Moet could not see her aggressor, the noise was
something that had instinctively raised the alarm. She had invaded
another's territory and if she didn't flee, the burning tear of claws
and fangs would be upon her. Moet cowered in submission. She
pressed her body flat and held back her ears as she attempted to
appease the tom. She inched backwards, away in the direction
of the nice garden. Again, came his scary song and a long hiss.
She shuffled backwards a little faster; belly still pressed against
the ground for protection. The yowl didn't get any closer, but he

continued to voice his displeasure angrily. After endless minutes, Moet turned around and staggered as fast as her starving belly and weak legs would carry her, bumping into walls and fenceposts on her way. She slowed down once the awful racket had stopped and flopped to the floor. He had not followed her, but her fur was still fluffed up like a brush and her ears flitted around listening for any trace of pursuit. Perhaps the tom had spared Moet on seeing her petite stature, starved frame and unkempt appearance. She would be a minimal threat to his kingdom.

Moet lifted her head. It rocked a little from side to side and she winced and blinked her blank eyes several times. With what seemed like her last fight, she put one paw in front of another, slowly and deliberately. She moved along the remainder of the row of doorways until she could smell the grass. She crawled in and collapsed by the bush.

What seemed like hours of fitful sleep later, there was a distant clip-clop. She cocked her head intently. As the footsteps grew louder, she tried to crawl under the bush for cover, but she could no longer move. Her body had given up on her and begged her to return to the world of sleep. The footsteps reached the doorway. Surely, she was now going to be shooed away, but there was nothing she could do.

The lady fumbled for her keys in her bag and just as she inserted the key into the lock, something caught the corner of her eye. Who had left that dirty grey rag by her shrubs? She stooped down to pick it up and put it in the bin and as she did, she let out a gasp of horror! Far from being a dirty, grey rag, she was horrified to see that it was an emaciated cat, filthy and motionless. Was it dead? The lady placed a hand on the cat's belly and let out a huge sigh as the skinny belly moved slowly and laboriously up and down.

Moet had moved her ears slightly at the gasp but did not react. She waited for the inevitable shove of rejection or rough hands. But they didn't come. Instead, gentle hands first touched her belly and then caressed her dirty fur. She lay perfectly still, responding only with a small raspy hint of a purr. The lady gently lifted Moet up and cradled her in her arms. Moet was then to feel something she had never felt in her short life, love. Those caring human hands who had reached in for Moet's littermates months ago were here. For her. Though she could no longer move, she continued to purr gently and relaxed into the lady's arms as she was carried inside.

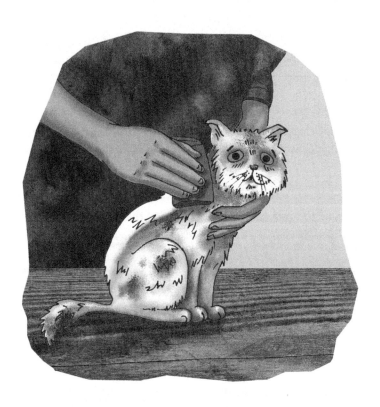

Once inside the house, Moet was placed on a soft cushion as the lady rushed about making lots of clattering noises and exclamations. After several minutes, a small dish of chicken broth was placed next to Moet with a few pieces of mashed up chicken. Moet lifted her fuzzy head slowly. The aroma of food wafted through from the kitchen. She could barely lift her head to sample it and the lady gently placed a small spoonful to Moet's lips. She lapped tentatively. Still weak, she simply lifted her head towards the lady and purred. The lady offered a small piece of chicken and Moet ate it with great effort. "There, that's enough for now", the lady said to Moet kindly. "Rest now and you can have some more later."

Chapter 4

Moet slept soundly, twitching her paws and ears every now and then as she drifted into dreaming sleep. When she woke with a start, the lady was right there, with more strokes and another plate of the chicken and a fresh dish of water. Moet ate and drank a little and then collapsed back down onto the cushion.

The lady busied herself again and returned with a bowl of warm water, a soft flannel and a towel. She lifted Moet gently and placed her on the towel. Soaking the flannel in the warm water, she started to wash Moet's grey fur. As she sponged her carefully, the grey fur started to change colour and the lady realised Moet was actually a beautiful cream colour with little darker patches on her head and back. She continued to wash, wiping the crusts from her sightless eyes and cleaning gently inside her ears. She then wrapped Moet in the towel to dry her and only then did she see Moet's cloudy eyes staring blankly around. She waved a hand in front of Moet's eyes, but there was no reaction. It was then that the lady realised Moet was blind. "What an amazing kitty you are, to have made it so far," she said to Moet. She kissed her head and cuddled her to her chest. Moet started to purr loudly and nuzzled into the towel. Never before had she experienced such care, love and tenderness.

As the evening went on, the lady put out a box and placed the cushion inside. Placing Moet into the box, she took her into a different room. There was a litter tray, a dish of tasty food and a bowl of water. The door closed and Moet was alone. Although the room was new and unfamiliar, Moet laid down in the box and immediately fell asleep.

When she woke the next morning, the kind lady first brought more food and after Moet had eaten, she stroked Moet's fur and left the room. Moet sniffed around the room and explored a little more, stretched and then settled down for a nap next to the box on the cool floor. But the lady returned minutes later with a carry box and lifted Moet gently into it. Moet seemed alarmed and her fur stood on end. The only thing Moet could associate with carriers was the pet shop. She held her head low and shrank back into corner of the box, the fight leaving her. She wanted to stay with this nice lady.

The lady walked out of the house, placing Moet into the front seat of her car. She reached across for the seatbelt. It stretched awkwardly around the box and made a reassuring click into the clasp. The car door closed, and the lady got into the other side. The noise and the motion put Moet to sleep but she woke when the car stopped, and the door again opened. The lady picked up the carrying box with Moet still huddled into one corner inside and walked into a place that smelled of animals.

She cowered lower into the box when placed onto a metal table and another set of hands reached in for her. Moet didn't struggle, and even let out a cursory purr, at least, until these unfamiliar hands started prodding and poking and putting a thermometer in her bum. The two ladies talked at length, both intermittently stroking Moet's head and the vet prodded gently around her eyes as she explained. Moet was approximately eleven months old and had 'cat flu' and that is what had stolen her sight. Although the vet didn't know how long she had been blind, she estimated that it would have been from between three and six months old – time enough for her to have caught the cat flu whilst in the pet shop and for the illness to have developed and caused the slow but eventual loss of sight. But she was not only blind, but very sick, half-starved and her eyes at risk of decaying and causing her further infection. She could, however, be nursed back to health, although she would have to stay at the vets for at least a week.

Moet shrank back against her carry box as the kind lady went to leave. Her ears were pressed against her head and her claws dug into the towel. The vet prised her carefully away and Moet hissed – a small pathetic hiss but a warning, nevertheless. The vet didn't react and continued to lift Moet and gently placed her into a cage with a blanket, a full bowl of food, a dish of fresh water and some toys. Moet's ears stood up again and her stance relaxed a little. Then came an injection that made her wince and shrink back into the corner of the cage. The 'IV', though clearly uncomfortable, would, said the vet, "make you feel better and get you strong again." Moet tugged at the bandage holding the needle in place but to no avail. She scratched and licked, but it wouldn't budge. Eventually she curled up awkwardly, shifted positions several times and stuck her paw out straight as the rest of her lay down for a nap.

It was hard to sleep with all the activity going on around her. Humans coming and going with cats, dogs and even birds and other small animals, making for a noisy day.

Once things eventually went quiet and the people stopped coming in with their various pets, another kind lady came to Moet's cage and opened the door, gave her some fresh food and stroked her cheeks. Moet purred and purred and was told what a happy and good kitty she was. After a little gentle playtime, for which she had limited energy still, she settled down to sleep for the night.

When she woke up, the magic fluid coming through the needle had clearly done its job. She could stand easily and ate a good breakfast She even hunched over a catnip toy and bunny-kicked it as well as she could with an IV line. As the days passed Moet got stronger and stronger and the vet said she was getting fatter.

After a few days, she was lifted out of the cage and told she was going in for 'surgery'. Moet was given an injection that made her fall asleep very quickly. When she woke up, she moved heavily and groggily and pawed at her eyes. She didn't get very far thanks to an awkward plastic cone they had placed around her neck. The collar made it impossible to do all manner of things, from having a good scratch to washing behind her ears and Moet became increasingly frustrated as she bumped into things and got the pesky thing stuck here, there, and everywhere in her cage .

Chapter 5

Moet started to explore more of the vet clinic. Every day after hours, she was allowed to roam around one of the rooms so that she could stretch her legs and be a little more active. She no longer had to wear the collar and the stitches in her eyes had been removed after five days. She was getting stronger, playing with the toys that were offered, jumping and pouncing around the room even once jumping high enough to hit her head on the underneath of a shelf. It was a minor bump and the jumps took place in a different part of the room after that. She was a quick learner and also a happy girl, who thrived on attention. Moet would raise a gentle paw to a leg to signal playtime or to beg for some of the delicious chicken that had been cooked up for all of the 'residents' as a treat. Each night she was returned to her cage and each morning as she was given her food, people talked about adoption, good homes and what a wonderful companion Moet would make.

And then came a familiar voice. She lifted her head in the direction of the voice. It was the lady who had brought her in. The cage door opened, and hands reached in to lift her down to the floor. The lady knelt next to her and stroked Moet's cheeks and rubbed her belly and even gave her a kiss. Moet purred loudly and kneaded gently on the lady's hands. "Come on sweet girl, I'm taking you home."

It had come. Her very own human and her very own home. She continued to purr as the lady, who was called Emily, placed her into a carry box and took Moet to her car.

As they travelled along together, Emily talked to Moet gently and told her tales of the things they would do, the fun they would have and the endless cuddles that awaited. Moet just lay in the carrier purring and sniffing the air, ears pricking up at the sound of Emily's voice. Once inside her new home, Emily put Moet into a room with everything she needed; food, water, litter box, scratching posts and so many toys and beds, she couldn't choose between them! Emily left Moet alone to get settled and familiarise herself with the room. Moet wandered around, sniffing every corner and object, pawing at things, batting toys here and there, sharpening her claws on the scratching posts and testing out every luxurious bed. Emily eventually returned with some fresh chicken and they sat together while Moet ate. Afterwards Emily sat in a chair and Moet waited next to her feet until she lifted Moet into her lap. Moet purred as her chin was rubbed, cheeks stroked, paws caressed, and head kissed. She settled into Emily's arms and together they fell asleep.

Chapter 6

Moet had settled so quickly into her new home and her new life. She and Emily had bonded almost instantly , although it took a few weeks before her and Luna, Emily's first rescue cat, became friends. At first Luna was hissy and stand-offish, being put out at having to share 'her' mum with Moet. But eventually, Luna enjoyed the company of a new friend when Emily went out to work each day. Although they were never going to snuggle up together and wile away the hours grooming each other, Luna did occasionally give Moet a cuddle and cursory lick.

She had been in her forever home for about four months when Emily decided it was time to start creating memories and a record of how Moet grew each day in confidence and skill. How she learned to play, run around the house, and jump up on things. She amazed Emily every day with her zest for life. Out came the camera. Moet often turned her head away from the camera or wandered off to sit elsewhere, seemingly irritated at the constant clicking following her around. But soon she would just listen intently and might even strike the odd random photo-worthy pose. Though she would never sit still for very long. Posing definitely wasn't her thing and as for clothes and accessories – no way!

Moet was definitely cute, but hard to photograph with no eyes. Look at any cat photograph and the thing that pulls you in is usually a pair of beautiful and mesmerising eyes. Still, the photos turned out well and the library was growing. But what to do with all of these pictures? Then it occurred to Emily that social media was the answer. She busied herself setting up Moet's social media pages: Instagram, Facebook, Twitter. Those would do for now. Up went the photos and captions, and very soon Moet was gaining followers. But more than that, Emily was gaining connections, friendships and having fun. People and pet accounts seemed to love Moet's sweet eyeless fluffy face and had endless questions about how she managed daily life. Did she play, did she use the litter box, could she find her food, and did she jump on the bed? Over the months that followed, Emily knew that Moet could do more on social media than simply being a 'presence'. Her blindness was attracting curiosity and interest and Moet could so easily start to raise awareness of blind cats in the hope that more were adopted from shelters. She could educate and help people to realise that blind cats are very capable and, in many ways, just like sighted cats. Of course, they may need a little extra care when it comes to safety and their environment, but watching her two cats, Emily realised they weren't really that different.

Chapter 7

Emily was also part of a volunteer group called 'Omani Paws'. The group, based in Oman, carries out 'TNR' (trap-neuter-return) for stray cats, helps any strays that are injured, rescues those that have been abandoned, neglected or abused and also helps to rehome as many cats and dogs as possible. Some members of the group foster a huge number of animals while they are waiting to be adopted and they work hard to make sure that any adoptions are permanent and that the animals are going to 'good' forever homes. Eventually the group expanded their activities to help with the import and export of pets for those people coming into the country or leaving. However, all of this was done without funding.

Because there is no animal welfare legislation in Oman, there is no government or official funding, no shelters and no animal charities (they are not permitted) and animals are not regarded highly. The feral cats and dogs are left unchecked to breed and the population continues to grow and, inevitably, to suffer, with little food and harsh weather conditions and even being abused, poisoned or shot by uncaring humans. Furthermore, the local cats are not well liked. Known as the Arabian Mau, and often highly prized in other countries for their intelligence, affection, health and playfulness, they are not desired by many locally. The prized pets are the 'Persians'; the generic name given in Oman to pretty much all long-haired cats, even when many may be other breeds. These long-haired (and sometimes the British Shorthair or Scottish Fold) cats, are usually only obtained through pet shops; like the one Moet came from.

Many of the pet shops are appalling. Cats, dogs and other animals cramped into small wire-floored cages with sparse food and water, no toys, no bedding, filthy surroundings and dirty litter trays. And while Moet was rescued, many are not and will suffer a worse fate if they get sick – being put out onto the streets in the fierce heat to either starve, be run over or be attacked by humans or other animals. The lucky ones who are adopted are sometimes abandoned when they cease to be fluffy kittens, are too much 'trouble', they get sick or when their owners leave the country to repatriate. This happens far too often, and Omani Paws picks up the pieces as best they can, relying on public generosity with donations of time, money and items to sell. But it's an uphill struggle and there are many times when vet bills get so high that they simply cannot help the next cat or dog that has been injured and desperately needs them.

So, Emily channelled much of her passion for rescue into the group, focussing mainly what she is good at – marketing, helping to write things and also donating items to sell regularly as well as her own funds when she can. But here's where Moet came in. With her growing social following, Emily decided to set up an online store with Moet merchandise and each year a Moet photo calendar. Every penny of the profits from the store sales are donated to Omani Paws. Emily had to work hard to try and grow Moet's following and ramp up the sales. Slowly, slowly, the followers grew and while there weren't huge volumes, she remains hopeful that one day Moet will hit the 'big time' so that much more can be donated, and many more animals can be helped.

Moet also uses 'her' voice on social media to raise awareness of the volunteer group and the plight of animals in Oman. One day, Emily hopes the situation here will be different, but for now, as a team, Moet and her mum will keep doing their thing to highlight the situation and make a difference to those without a voice, who are so desperate for their helping paws and hands. And who knows, if they make enough from their ventures, Emily's dream may well come true; to open Oman's first ever cat shelter.

Printed in Great Britain
by Amazon

24428330R00020